WHAT IS A TRIANGLE?

by REBECCA KAI DOTLICH
photographs by MARIA FERRARI

HarperFestival®
A Division of HarperCollinsPublishers

A candy corn,
a chocolate kiss,

a sandwich cut
in shapes like this.

An ice cream cone,
the point of a star,

the colorful top of a cookie jar.
The tip of an arrow,

a birthday hat,

two pieces of pie
sliced nice and fat.

A kitty cat's ear,

the roof on a house,
a soft wedge of cheese for a hungry mouse.

A triangle, a turnover,

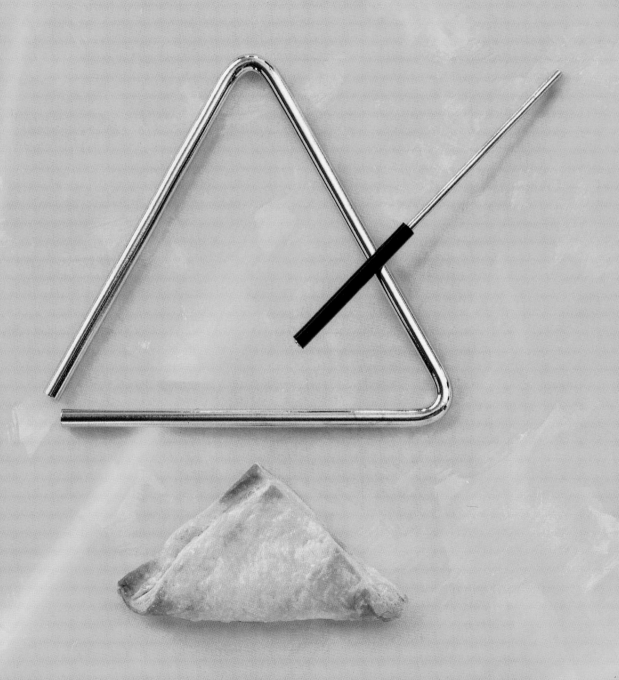

a block, a tree,

a boat with a sail
on the big blue sea.

A part of a kite,

and a paper plane,

a colorful link
in a plastic chain.

A bright folded napkin,
a teddy bear's nose,

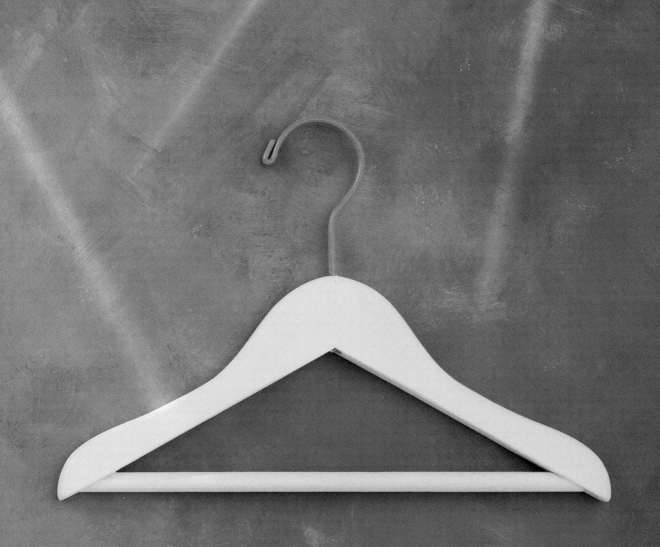

the part of a hanger
that wears your clothes.

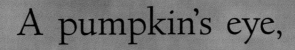
A pumpkin's eye,

pizza sliced in a pan. . . .

Can you find a TRIANGLE?